# Puss in Boots

A Fairy Tale by Charles Perrault
Retold and supplemented with necessary
explanations and illustrations by Hans Fischer

Translated by Anthea Bell · Afterword by Hans ten Doornkaat

North-South Books · New York · London

ONCE UPON A TIME there was a miller who died and left his mill, his donkey, and his cat to his three sons. When they shared out the property, the eldest son took the mill, the second son had the donkey, and the third son was left with nothing but the cat. He felt very sad. "My brothers can earn a good living working together with the mill and the donkey," he said. "But what am I to do with a cat? Once I've eaten him and made his fur into a warm cap, I'll starve to death!"

Puss, however, was no ordinary cat. "Cheer up!" he told his master. "Just have a pair of boots made for me, and give me a sack with strings at the top to close it, and you'll find you're not so badly off after all."

The miller's son didn't know what to think of that, but he knew Puss was a clever cat, so he took him to the shoemaker's and had him measured for a pair of boots.

*What the story doesn't say is that it is not easy for a cat to stand up and walk on his hind legs wearing boots. Puss had to learn in secret, by night: first he learned to stand and then he learned to walk and in the end he could do it very well!*

When Puss could walk on his hind legs, he took his sack off to the vegetable garden. He pulled up a few carrots and picked some fresh cabbage leaves, put them in the sack, and went hunting rabbits.

Out in the forest, he lay down and waited until a silly young rabbit came along. The rabbit saw the carrots and cabbage leaves in the sack, and jumped inside to eat them.

Puss pulled the strings tight, trapping the rabbit. He slung the sack over his shoulder, took it to the palace, and asked to see the king. Bowing low, he said, "Your Majesty, this rabbit is a present from the Marquis of Carabas." (That was the name he had made up for his master.)

The next day he put some grain in his sack, went to a wheat field, lay down, and waited for partridges.

A fat partridge soon came along to eat the grain. Puss pulled the sack shut and hurried off to give the partridge to the king.

Like all cats, Puss was good at fishing, and whenever he caught a particularly big fish he gave it to the king too.

Puss went on like this for several months, going hunting or fishing every day and taking his catch to the king. He always made a deep bow and said, "My master, the Marquis of Carabas, sends you this present."

The king enjoyed the rabbits, partridges, and fish very much. He grew fatter and happier day by day, and he thought the Marquis of Carabas must be a very fine fellow.

One day Puss heard that the king was going out in the royal coach with his daughter, and would drive past the lake.

"Take my advice," he told his master, "and your fortune is made! All you have to do is swim in this lake. Just leave the rest to me."

By now the miller's son was used to following his cat's advice, so he took off his clothes and jumped into the water.

Meanwhile, Puss hid the young man's clothes under a big rock. No sooner had he hidden them than the royal coach came driving by.

"Help! Help!" shouted Puss. "My master's drowning!"

The king heard him, recognized the cat who brought him such nice things to eat, made the coachman stop, and told his servants to pull the young man out of the lake.

Puss said his master's clothes had been stolen, so the king sent a servant back to the palace to fetch some of his best clothes for the Marquis of Carabas. The miller's son put on the fine clothes, and they suited him very well. Now at least he looked like a marquis! The king invited the young man to join him and his daughter on their drive, offering him a seat next to the princess, who liked that very much.

*What the story doesn't say is that Puss had been trying out some terrible faces in front of a mirror. For the first time ever, we show him doing it here. And you'll soon find out why!*

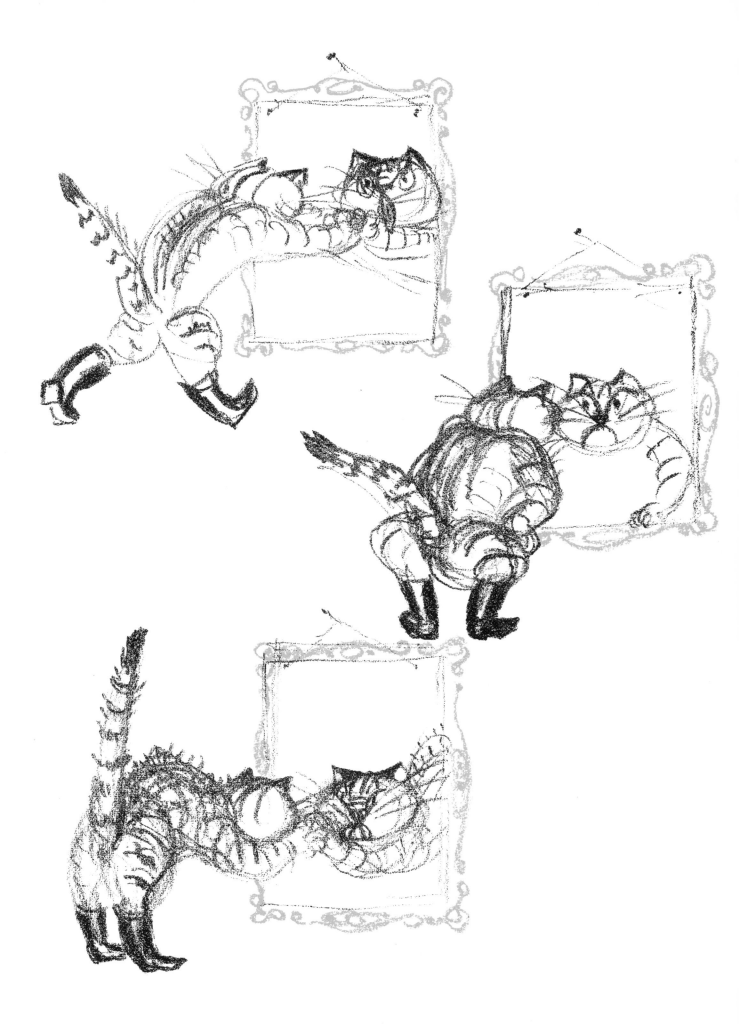

However, Puss ran on ahead of the royal coach, and came to a great meadow where some men were making hay. "Listen, haymakers!" he said. "When the king drives by and asks who owns this meadow, you must say it belongs to the Marquis of Carabas. If you don't, you'll all be made into mincemeat!" And he made a really terrible face.

Soon the king came driving by and asked the haymakers, "Who owns this fine meadow?"

"It belongs to the Marquis of Carabas!" they all cried, because they were terrified of Puss.

The king congratulated the marquis on owning such a fine meadow. The miller's son just smiled modestly, and the king thought, "What a noble marquis he is!"

Puss in Boots ran on ahead again, and he came to a great field where some men were reaping wheat. "Listen, reapers!" he said. "When the king drives by and asks who owns this wheat, you must say it belongs to the Marquis of Carabas. If you don't, you'll all be made into mincemeat!"

Soon afterwards, the king came driving by, and asked who owned the field of wheat.

"It belongs to the Marquis of Carabas!" said the reapers, who were terrified of the fierce cat. The king liked the marquis even better than before.

Puss in Boots ran on and on until he came to a castle belonging to a giant.

*What the story doesn't say is that Puss was just a little bit afraid of the giant, so he washed and brushed and groomed himself first, to keep up his courage.*

Puss had asked some questions in advance, and discovered that the giant was a great magician and enormously rich. He owned all the fields and forests through which the king was driving. Puss knocked on the castle gate and sent in a message, saying he couldn't pass the castle without paying his respects to the most famous magician in the world.

The giant could sometimes be very cross and nasty, but luckily he was in high spirits when Puss was shown in. He was just trying some new magic tricks, and he always enjoyed that.

Puss was glad to find the giant in a good mood. He immediately started talking about magic. "I've been told you can change your shape better than any other magician in the world," he said.

"Quite true!" said the giant. "Look at my picture gallery! I can turn into all these different animals!" He was a very vain giant, and liked to have his portrait painted in all kinds of shapes. "What would you like me to turn into?" he asked.

"An elephant!" said Puss.

The next moment the giant had turned into an elephant, and he let Puss swing on his trunk.

"This is fun!" said Puss—but suddenly there was a great roar, and the giant had turned into a lion! "Wonderful!" cried Puss, although he was dreadfully scared. "But can you turn into an animal as small as a mouse?"

"Nothing easier!" roared the lion. The next moment he was gone, and there was only a tiny mouse scampering over the floor. Just what Puss was waiting for! He pounced, caught the mouse, and ate it up.

By now the king's coach had reached the magician's castle. Puss came out to meet the visitors in the courtyard. "Your Majesty," he said solemnly, "welcome to the castle of my master, the Marquis of Carabas!" The king admired the castle very much, for it was even larger and finer than his palace. Puss showed the whole company into the great hall, where he had a banquet ready, prepared by the magician's servants and animals. They were much happier working for Puss than for the wicked giant.

The king was in a very good mood. He ate and drank heartily, and since the Marquis of Carabas was so rich and owned so much land, and the princess and the marquis were getting on very well together, their wedding was held at once. As the day drew to a close, they all went on celebrating with music and dancing by moonlight.

*What the story doesn't say is that Puss was very, very glad when he could take his boots off at last!*

# HANS FISCHER

HANS FISCHER, who was known by his trademark signature, *fis,* was one of the most popular Swiss illustrators in the years following World War II, and an important influence in the field of children's book illustration throughout the world.

He was born in Berne, Switzerland, in 1909 and attended the School of Fine and Industrial Arts in Geneva, the School of Arts and Crafts in Zurich, and the Fernand Léger Academy in Paris, France. He worked as an illustrator, an advertising artist and graphic designer, and a stage designer and set painter for the legendary Cabaret Cornichon in Zurich. He was also well known as a muralist, and his bright, animated works still decorate the walls of public buildings all over Switzerland.

Fischer became famous for his illustrations of cats. They played a large role in all of his work and are featured prominently in his children's books, including two that he created as gifts for his own children, *The Birthday* and *Pitschi.* It is therefore not surprising that his American editor, Margaret K. McElderry, then of Harcourt Brace in New York, suggested to Fischer that he do a picture book version of Charles Perrault's classic fairy tale *Puss in Boots.* At first the project appealed to Fischer, but when he began to work on it, he ran into difficulties. In his journal, under a sketch showing Puss on the ground (having fallen while learning to walk in boots), Fischer wrote, "This isn't going easily. The cat is on his belly—as is Hans Fischer!" In a lecture he delivered that same year, Fischer explained part of the problem, saying, "I prefer to work with projects that are not commissioned, but are instead my own creations, especially when it comes to children's books and graphic art. There I can recreate my favorite plants and animals, and memories from my childhood return—from my bird and fish period. (I'm passionate about fishing—must be something about my last name.)"

Fischer felt that Perrault's Puss was an unsympathetic character and that the giant who appears at the end of the tale was far too scary. Eventually he decided to rework the text, shortening and modifying it. He made the giant's magic tricks far more playful, and humorously exaggerated the flaws of Puss's victims—the king's avarice, the giant's vanity—which helped make Puss seem less exploitative.

Fischer also transformed Puss himself, making him more human, more sympathetic, while at the same time retaining certain catlike traits—sneakiness and secretiveness. When Puss is nervous about going to meet the giant, he conquers his fear by grooming himself. Although he brushes his coat with a brush and comb, he shines his boots with his tongue. Fischer expanded on Puss's transformation from a four-legged creature to a two-legged one, showing just how hard this was for the hero. Similarly, in a series of brilliant illustrations, Fischer shows Puss learning to make intimidating faces.

By changing the story, Fischer was able to incorporate his own lifelong themes of change and playfulness, which allowed him to move ahead with the project. After weeks of exhausting work on the text, he wrote in his journal, "Finally, this is coming to life! (My playful instincts have been awakened!)"

*Puss in Boots* is a perfect example of Hans Fischer's mastery of stone lithography, a printmaking process more commonly used for fine art than for illustration. He drew the art directly onto large stones—one for each color—which the Swiss printer Eduard Wolfensberger personally delivered to his home. The book was published in autumn 1957 in Switzerland in a limited edition with original lithographs signed by the illustrator. At the same time, a less expensive edition was printed on an offset press.

Sadly, Fischer never saw the Harcourt Brace edition, because on April 18, 1958, he died of heart failure. Just a few months before his death he had mailed out New Year's cards with a drawing of Puss with his chin on his paws. Under this thoughtful picture of his alter ego he wrote the year 1958 and the question: "How will it be?"

*Hans ten Doornkaat*

First North-South Books edition published in 1996.
Copyright © 1966 by Nord-Süd Verlag AG, Gossau Zürich, Switzerland.
First published in Switzerland under the title *Der gestiefelte Kater*
English translation copyright © 1996 by North-South Books Inc.

Published in the United States, Great Britain, Canada,
Australia, and New Zealand by North-South Books, an imprint
of Nord-Süd Verlag AG, Gossau Zürich, Switzerland.

Distributed in the United States by North-South Books Inc., New York.

Library of Congress Cataloging-in-Publication Data is available.
A CIP catalogue record for this book is available from The British Library.

*For more information about our books, and the authors and artists
who create them, visit our web site:* http://www.northsouth.com

ISBN 1-55858-642-3 (TRADE BINDING)
1 3 5 7 9 TB 10 8 6 4 2
ISBN 1-55858-643-1 (LIBRARY BINDING)
1 3 5 7 9 LB 10 8 6 4 2
Printed in Germany